About the Author
Ji Hyun Lee studied Chinese literature in college. Her books include: *I Wonder Who Lives Next Door, My Runaway Dog, The History of Our Pottery, If There Was a Tree in Our House, and The Very Beautiful Field,* among others.

About the Illustrator
Jin Hwa Kim studied communications in college. She has illustrated several books for children, including *I Need a Friend, I Love Cars, Dad is Always First Place, What is Your Dream?, Sparkling Healthy Eyes,* and others. She enjoys spending her spare time on Sundays with her dog. The illustrations for this book were created using paper carvings and collages to portray the feeling of warmth in homes.

Tantan Publishing Knowledge Storybook *Precious Home*

www.TantanPublishing.com

Published in the U.S. in 2017 by TANTAN PUBLISHING, INC.
4005 w Olympic Blvd., Los Angeles, CA 90019-3258

©Copyright 2017 by Dong-hwi Kim
English Edition

ISBN: 978-1-939248-19-0

Printed in Korea

Precious Home

Written by Ji Hyun Lee   Illustrated by Jin Hwa Kim

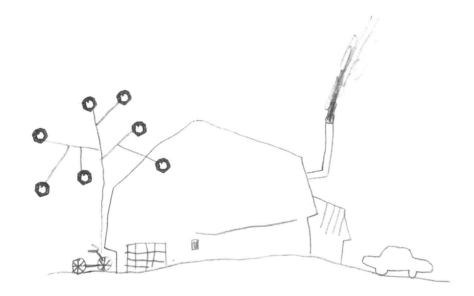

✿ TanTan Publishing

This is a house.
It is the house I live in.

Big house. Little house.
There are many kinds
of houses.

My house has a roof and walls.
The roof blocks the sunlight, and
protects me from snow and rain.
The walls keep the cold air out,
bringing warmth to everyone inside.

My house has a window and a door.
The window lets air into the house,
and brings the sunlight in.
The door makes it easier to enter and
leave the house.

In the house we can eat, sleep,
rest comfortably,
and wash our bodies.

I live in my house with my family.
We have a good time
doing things we like to do,
and feeling comfortable and safe.
Houses give people a feeling of happiness.

There are houses wherever people live.
All houses look different,
and all houses are built with different materials.
People in countries all around the world
live in different kinds of houses
that are built to fit their surroundings.

Some houses in Thailand are built on wooden poles.
Thailand is hot and humid, and it rains there all year long.
Occasionally, heavy rains even cause flooding.
So houses are built on wooden poles to
keep them above the water.

The stairs are used
to enter the house.

The space below the
house is used to raise
livestock or as storage.
Children can play there,
or adults can work there.

The roof is made by weaving tree leaves and grass together. It is built on a slant to let the heavy rains easily slide down.

The walls have many gaps because they are made from wooden boards or bamboo.
The wind flows through the house and keeps the house cool.

The doors and windows are built mostly to let in fresh air.

The wooden floors are raised off the ground to prevent moisture to prevent moisture from coming in.

Meals are made mostly from rice, vegetables, fish, and fruits.

There is a carpet on the floor made from woven bamboo and grass.

Even during heavy rainfall, the house does not flood because the house is built on top of high poles. This also keeps people safe from dangerous animals, such as snakes.

In Togo, a country in Africa, there are soil houses.
The sun beams down strongly in Togo, and it is very hot and dry because there is little rainfall.
Soil is easy to find, and building houses out of soil
keeps the house cool by blocking the hot sun's rays from coming through.

The roof is built by evenly spreading thick soil.
The roof is used to dry grains.

The pointy part of the roof is built by weaving straw and grass together.

There is a separate door for small livestock to enter and exit.

The walls are built by kneading mud upward into a cylinder shape.
Plastering cow manure and soil onto the walls prevents rain from leaking into the house.

The bedroom doors are built smaller to make it difficult for animals and outsiders to enter.

Small towers, one for each family member, are placed in front of the house to chase bad spirits away.

The bedrooms and kitchen are on the second floor.

There is a place to raise livestock on the first floor.

This is where grain is crushed

There is a small opening in the wall where you can peek outside. This opening lets in wind and sunlight.

The grain storage can be opened and closed through the rooftop. The storage area has dividers to separate the different kinds of grains.

In Mongolia, there are tent houses called gers.
Wide grasslands in Mongolia
make it a perfect place to raise livestock such as
sheep and horses.
People who raise livestock
migrate from place to place searching for grass.
Tent houses make moving convenient because
they are easy to assemble and take apart.

Gers are built low and round to
withstand the grassland's
strong winds.

The tent is covered in thick fabric
called felt.
Felt is made from wool and it keeps
wind from entering.

A leather strap tightly ties
down the ger to keep it
from blowing away.

The door of the house faces south to let in sunlight.

There is an opening in the middle of the roof.
It is the only window in a ger.
Sunlight comes in through this window,
and smoke from the stove
goes out through it.

There is a carpet on the
floor to block the cold air
coming up from the ground.

The wooden frame of the roof looks like the ribs of an umbrella.

Wooden sticks are woven together like a net to build the walls. These sticks are easily foldable.

There is a stove in the middle of the house. The stove keeps the house warm, and is also used to cook.

Horse milk is used to make many things, such as airag and cheese. Airag is a mild alcoholic drink.

In Russia, where the weather is
extremely cold,
some houses are built from
wooden logs.
Russia has many forests where
trees with thick, straight trunks,
such as pine and spruce,
are easily available.
Logs help block the cold air.
Houses built from logs are very
strong, and the house stays warm
during cold weather.

Shutters are
added to the
windows to
block the
cold air.

Logs are laid horizontally on top of
each other to create the walls.
The gaps between the logs are filled
with moss and wood pieces to keep
the cold air out.

This chimney lets out the smoke
that is made inside the house.

Wooden boards are pieced
together to make the roof.
The steeply tilted roof helps
the snow slide down so
it doesn't pile up.

This is a wooden bed.

A fire in the fireplace
keeps the house warm.
The fireplace can be used for
cooking or to dry wet laundry.

In Greenland, a country in the Arctic, there is
an ice house called an igloo.
The Inuit people who live in the region hunt
for fish and seals in the ocean.
Normally they live in wooden or brick houses,
but when they travel far to hunt,
they build igloos using readily available snow
and ice to escape from the cold.

Solid blocks of snow or
ice are cut into bricks
and stacked up in a
round shape.
Then the cracks are
filled with snow.
This way, the cold air
cannot get inside
the house.

The door is built low and narrow
to prevent cold air from entering.

A small opening on the top
lets air in and out.

Dome-shaped houses are sturdier
than square-shaped houses,
and make it easier for cold winds
to go around them.

After some snow blocks are
stacked on the floor,
they are covered with a thick
animal skin and used as a bed.

A leather covering is
spread on the floor to
block cold air coming up
from the ground.

Fire is lit using oil from whales or seals. The burning oil generates heat that warms up the house.

The house is not spacious because it is a temporary house.

There are houses wherever people live.
Even though houses have different
appearances in every country, each one is
someone's precious home.

A house built on wooden poles in Thailand

A mud house in Togo